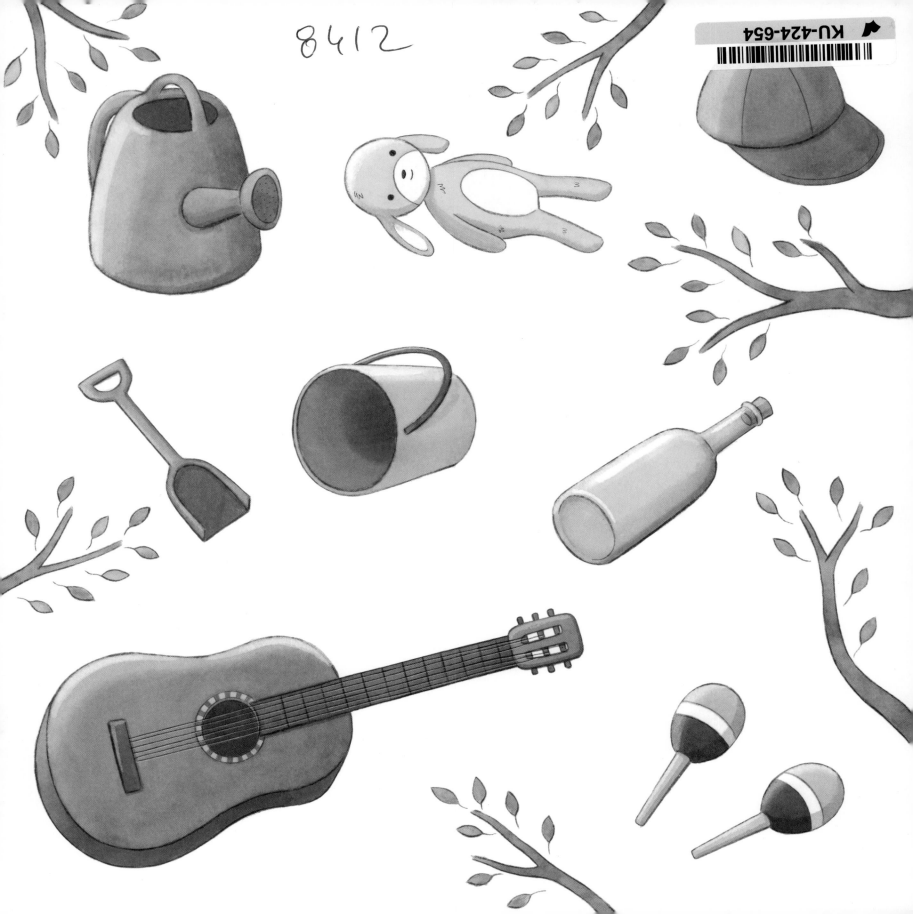

8412

In Our Hands

Lucy Farfort

Tate

We called it 'The Dulling'. It had been creeping in for such a long time, and had started so gradually, that most people barely even noticed.

Perhaps they didn't want to see.

No one knew what to do except carry on as normal,
as if we could ignore the problem away.

As The Dulling spread,
people felt sad and angry.
They blamed each other and
there were terrible arguments.

Hurt replaced harmony.
Neighbours became enemies.
But this didn't solve anything.

When the last drop of colour finally left our planet,
the people in charge shrugged their shoulders
and said nothing could be done.

Still, in my small corner of the world,
I kept my eyes open for answers.

Because you never knew
when out of the blue
the tiniest thing could show up
and spark a transformation.

Such as a single grain of hope,
found by those like us.

Dreamers with a gaze
that never quit...

At first it seemed like
nothing was happening.

So I shouted for help.

And someone heard my call.
"Hello!" he said.
"I've brought an idea."

And guess what? It worked.
"If we gather more people,
this could change things!" we cried.

Pop!

Most walked past without even stopping,
too busy to care.

Many had grown used to the grey.
"Learn to live with it!" they said.

This made us want to walk away,
but we kept each other going.

Bit by joyful bit, others took notice.
And everyone who joined, gave new energy.

There were some funny suggestions along the way,
but each offered the glint of a brighter tomorrow.

At times,

the effort was exhausting.

When things got really tough,

we had to work as one.

Then I woke one morning,
and the air felt different.
It was filled with the
smell of promise.

Like the flick of a switch our dream had blossomed,

and in front of us stood a beacon of hope!

I guess from a distance, amongst all that grey,
it must have appeared a speck of a change.

Yet we all knew deep down,
that together we'd started
something incredible.

And in our hands . . .

was the key,

to help others do the same.

for change, progression and hope,
and the brave ones lighting the way.

First published 2022 by order of the Tate Trustees
by Tate Publishing, a division of Tate Enterprises Ltd,
Millbank, London SW1P 4RG
www.tate.org.uk/publishing

Text and illustrations © Lucy Farfort 2022

Designer: Roanne Marner
Editor: Cherise Lopes-Baker
Production: Juliette Dupire

A catalogue record for this book is available from the British Library

ISBN 978 1 84976 814 6

Distributed in the United States and Canada by ABRAMS, New York
Library of Congress Control Number applied for

Colour reproduction by Evergreen Colour Management Ltd
Printed and bound in China by C&C Offset Printing Co, Ltd

FSC
www.fsc.org

MIX
Paper from
responsible sources
FSC® C008047